ATLANTIS
THE LOST EMPIRE
THE ESSENTIAL GUIDE

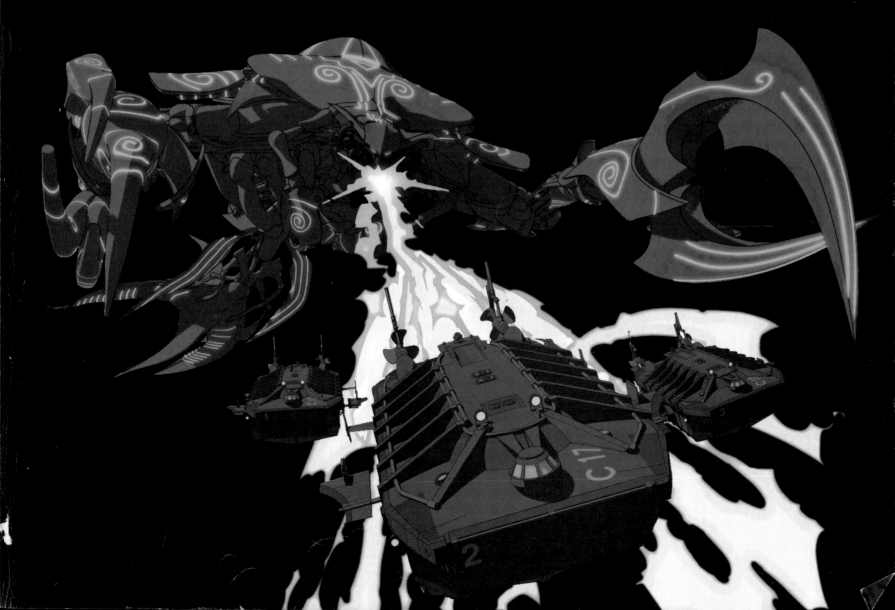

DISNEY'S
ATLANTIS
THE LOST EMPIRE
THE ESSENTIAL GUIDE

A Dorling Kindersley Book

Contents

How to read Atlantean

Match the Atlantean symbols in the word you are reading to those in the chart below and you will see their corresponding letter in English. Put the letters together to spell the word. For example, ⟐⟐⟐ = cat. Do the same for numbers. For numbers 11 and up put the symbol for each part of the number together. For example 12 (1 and 2) = ·⁝

CH	SH	TH

A	B	C	D	E	F	G	H	I	J	K	L	M

N	O	P	Q	R	S	T	U	V	W	X	Y	Z

1	2	3	4	5	6	7	8	9	10	0

FOREWORD

A utopian empire, the mother of all civilizations, vanishes from the face of the earth in one horrific, cataclysmic event. It's no wonder that Atlantis has been the center of fascination for centuries, and no wonder that the Disney Animators jumped at the chance to capture the Atlantis myth on film.

We knew that if we were going to transport the audience to this amazing place, we needed to tell a story that was full of compelling characters like Milo, Kida, Vinny, and Molière. But we also wanted to make a film full of awesome creatures, unimaginable vehicles, and heart-stopping action.

Along the way we created an entire universe of new mythology, starting with the rusty 1914 sheet-metal-and-rivets world of the explorers and culminating with the magical, colorful world of the Atlanteans, their language, and their culture. Dorling Kindersley has captured all this and more in the pages of this spectacular guide where it can be studied and appreciated for ages to come.

So sit back and let us be your guide to a whole new world.

Atlantis is waiting . . .

Don Hahn

DON HAHN
PRODUCER OF
ATLANTIS: THE LOST EMPIRE

THE LEGEND

THOUSANDS OF YEARS AGO, there was a prosperous empire called Atlantis. At the heart of the empire was a giant Crystal. Its energy was used to generate light and power, and to give the people long life.

Eventually the Atlanteans realized that they could use the Crystal's power to dominate other civilizations. But their plan backfired horribly when there was a huge explosion. The force created a massive tidal wave which headed straight for Atlantis itself.

The terrified Atlanteans ran for their lives, led by the king, queen, and their daughter Princess Kida. As Kida struggled to pick up her doll, a mysterious beam of red light came from the Crystal. It landed on the queen, and she was swept up into the air. She was never seen again. Seconds later the the tidal wave hit the island, and Atlantis disappeared below the stormy sea. Not a trace was left to show that it had ever existed. But somehow the empire survived beneath the water.

"...IN A SINGLE DAY AND NIGHT OF MISFORTUNE, THE ISLAND OF ATLANTIS DISAPPEARED INTO THE DEPTHS OF THE SEA"

– PLATO, 360 B.C.

AFTER Atlantis disappeared, the only clue to its location lay in a mysterious book, called The Shepherd's Journal. The Vikings managed to find it and embarked on a journey across the seas to find Atlantis. They did not appreciate the dangers that lay ahead. As they neared their destination, the tail of an enormous creature rose from the raging sea. Then, with one blast from the huge beast, the Viking fleet was destroyed. Everything sank slowly to the seabed. One Viking survived. But The Shepherd's Journal was lost....

MILO THATCH

IT IS NOW 1914, and a young man called Milo Thatch is working in the boiler room of a city museum. A talented cartographer and linguist, he dreams of becoming a great explorer. When he thinks he knows the location of *The Shepherd's Journal*, which maps the way to Atlantis, Milo gets very excited. But the museum's board refuses to fund an expedition to find the *Journal*. Milo thinks all is lost, until he is summoned to meet a wily old billionaire with an amazing proposition!

MILO *spends his days tending to the boiler in the basement of the city museum.*

Glasses

Thick, military coat

Leather satchel for carrying books and maps

THADDEUS THATCH

Milo's parents died when he was very small, so he was raised and educated by his explorer grandfather, Thaddeus Thatch. Though Thaddeus has passed away, Milo thinks of him constantly. He will never forget the wonder and excitement he felt when Grandpa Thatch recounted his expeditions.

Milo studies ancient languages and maps

"AH, *Sir! Wait, Mr. Harcourt! Sir, I...I have new evidence that...*" *shouts Milo. It's clear that the museum's director does not want to hear any more time-wasting folklore about Atlantis!*

Jodhpur-style pants

Waterproof leg protectors

SURPRISE SURPRISE!
When Milo comes home from the museum, he is surprised to find a mysterious blonde in his living room. Helga has been sent to take him to see the billionaire industrialist Mr. Whitmore. He has an intriguing proposition for Milo.

WITHIN days of meeting Mr. Whitmore, Milo is on board the ship the Lewis and Clark *bound for the adventure of a lifetime. But he doesn't have the stomach for sea travel and is violently sick over the railings!*

THE ship's crew is not always impressed with Milo's bumbling accounts of myths, legends, and the like. They do not all share his love of the unknown.

BOILER MAN
Milo's knowledge of boilers doesn't go to waste. When one of the vehicles breaks down, Milo sees that its boiler is similar to the one at the museum. With a few tweaks to the motor and a whack with the wrench, he gets it going again—much to his crewmate's surprise!

Explorer's hat

RISKY BUSINESS
When Thaddeus was a young man, large areas of the world were still unexplored. For centuries, Western mapmakers had to leave Africa blank on world maps because it was such an unknown place. Missionaries like David Livingstone risked their lives exploring the great rivers of central Africa.

Explorers often returned home with artifacts, like this ancient spear

SCOTT'S DISAPPOINTMENT
In 1911, the conquest of the South Pole was one of the few challenges left for explorers. Norwegian explorer Roald Amundsen (1872–1928) and British explorer Sir Robert Scott (1868–1912) (*above*) both led teams to reach it. Amundsen's team got there first, much to Scott's disappointment.

HELGA SINCLAIR

HELGA SINCLAIR is a cold, beautiful blonde with a shady background. Born to a German mother and a Scottish father, Helga was the oldest of six children, and the only girl. Her father encouraged her natural athletic ability, and she went on to study small arms combat and martial arts to instructor level. Helga later had training in firearms under a soldier called Rourke. Her expertise and intelligence impressed him. Rourke also saw her potential as a spy, and she joined him on an expedition to Egypt as his intelligence officer. She now works for Mr. Whitmore as his bodyguard and chauffeur.

"DON'T drip on the Caravaggio," Helga tells Milo at Whitmore's mansion. In the elevator she straightens his tie. She clearly finds him a bit pathetic!

CHESS EXPERT

Helga is an expert at chess, a board game that has been around for thousands of years. Variations of the game were first played in both India and China. The board originally represented a field in battle in which players captured enemy soldiers.

POWERFUL LADY

Helga's charisma, aggressive nature, and intelligence make her an excellent trainer and enforcer. She is the muscle behind Rourke's orders. Rourke appreciates Helga's abilities only too well. After all, she is one of only three living people to have beaten him at unarmed combat and chess!

MATA HARI

Mata Hari (1876–1917) was a famous Dutch spy during World War I, about the same time as Helga. She was a dancer in France when she was recruited by the German Secret Service. However, she didn't make a very good spy and they did not entirely trust her. Germany finally betrayed her to France. She was executed by a French firing squad in 1917.

HELGA remains cool in a crisis. She thinks and acts quickly in the face of danger.

PERFECT PARTNER

Following the meeting with Mr. Whitmore, Helga joins Milo on his trip. She is in her element giving orders to the crew. She has a sharp, analytical mind, which is perfect for campaign planning.

Skilled drill instructor

Hair tied back in a braid

MR. *Whitmore has issued Helga a stylish car: the Dorfenheimer Wildcat. Such an expensive vehicle just adds to Helga's mystique.*

Accomplished in many types of martial arts

Gun holster

Custom-made military pants

HELGA'S *a cool beauty with an aloof, edgy exterior. She is calculating, determined, and ultimately ruthless. Love and romance have no appeal for her. The pursuit of power and money is her only real passion.*

AS *the crew steers toward their final destination, they do not know that Rourke and Helga have a secret plan. When Helga's conscience briefly troubles her, Rourke soon changes her mind.*

HELGA *is quite a fighter. With her father's encouragement, by the age of 12 she was a challenging sparring partner and had mastered the art of knife throwing and target shooting.*

HELGA *proves she is made of tough stuff. When fighting for her life she shows that she has catlike reflexes and sharp martial arts moves.*

It's dark and rainy as Helga drives Milo through the giant iron gates to Preston Whitmore's mansion. Once inside, Milo stares at his surroundings in wonder. The house is full of rare and priceless artifacts that have been collected from all over the world. What on earth could the owner of such a mansion want with Milo?

PRESTON B. WHITMORE

MILO MAY HAVE FELT a little uneasy about meeting the eccentric billionaire industrialist, but Mr. Whitmore greets him with warmth, kindness, and a foot to shake! Milo can barely contain his excitement when Mr. Whitmore presents him with the long lost *Shepherd's Journal*. Amazingly, Mr. Whitmore has financed and gathered an impressive expedition force to find Atlantis. Now, with Milo to translate the *Journal*, the full crew is assembled. The search for the lost city can begin.

"IT's a pleasure to meet you, Milo. Join me in a little yoga?" asks Mr. Whitmore, offering Milo a foot to shake!

Spiky hair

Rare, Indian seat cover

Joints crack loudly during yoga

Walking stick

Ancient chair from Africa

IT turns out that Mr. Whitmore made a bet with Milo's grandfather, Thaddeus. *"I said, 'Thatch, if you ever actually find that so-called Journal, not only will I finance the expedition, I'll kiss ya full on the mouth.' Imagine my embarrassment when he found the darn thing."*

THE WAY TO TRAVEL

"I will find Atlantis on my own! If I have to rent a rowboat!" exclaims Milo in his excitement. This is exactly what Mr. Whitmore wants to hear. He pushes a button, and the table in front of them opens to reveal miniature models of an expedition convoy. "Forget the rowboat, son. We'll travel in style."

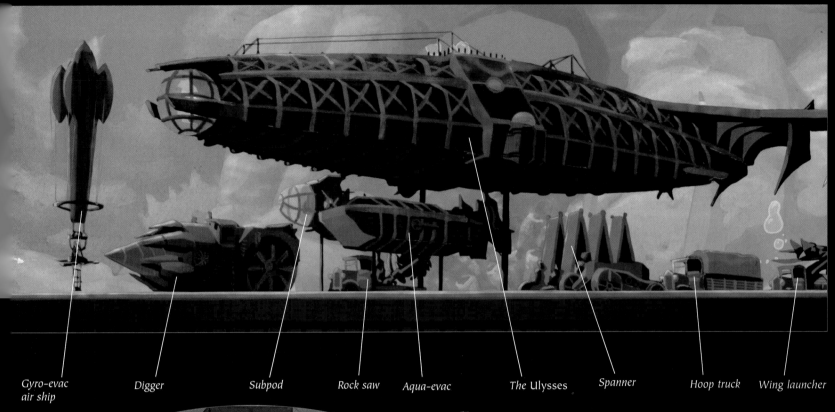

Gyro-evac air ship	Digger	Subpod	Rock saw	Aqua-evac	The Ulysses	Spanner	Hoop truck	Wing launcher

EVEN though Thaddeus is gone, Mr. Whitmore has remained true to his word. He's financed and built a secret expedition task force, the likes of which have never been seen before. Thaddeus Thatch would have been delighted!

THE JOURNEY BEGINS

Mr. Whitmore, crossing his fingers for luck, waves goodbye as the sub starts its descent. "Make us proud, boy!" he calls after Milo. He knows that there is no telling what the crew may encounter on the journey to the murky depths.

PAVING THE WAY

Many eccentric billionaires have financed projects and given lots of money to charity, just like Mr. Whitmore. The famous American banker John Pierpont Morgan (1837–1913) (*right*) was one such billionaire. During his lifetime he contributed to art museums, cathedrals, churches, and hospitals. After his death the Metropolitan Museum of Art in New York City received a large part of Morgan's collection.

THE crew that Mr. Whitmore has assembled is indeed "the best of the best." It was the team that helped Thaddeus recover The Shepherd's Journal *from Iceland.*

Yoga pose

YOGA

Mr. Whitmore came across yoga on an expedition to India. Yoga is a system of meditation, relaxation, and exercise that is very calming.

THE JOURNAL

*T*HE *SHEPHERD'S JOURNAL* is the key to finding Atlantis.

The small book is written on parchment and is beautifully decorated with golden letters. It is written entirely in Atlantean, which when translated gives the exact location of and map to Atlantis. The *Journal* has had a long history. It has passed through many countries and civilizations over the centuries—a small shard of Atlantean crystal in the cover ensures it remains intact. The book has been hidden for years. Then, on an expedition to Iceland by Thaddeus Thatch, the mysterious *Journal* is unearthed.

Milo could not believe it when Mr. Whitmore handed him The Shepherd's Journal. *It had been in Iceland all along, just as he'd suspected.*

Egyptian hieroglyphs

WRITE LIKE AN EGYPTIAN

Milo managed to decode written Atlantean using his knowledge of other languages. This is how Egyptian hieroglyphics were finally translated, too. On an ancient stone, called the Rosetta Stone, was written a thank you letter to an Eygptian ruler. It had been written in three ancient languages including hieroglyphs and Greek. By using the Greek script, the hieroglyphs could be decoded.

ANCIENT LANGUAGE

Milo quickly found similarities between Atlantean and the ancient languages of Greek, Hebrew, Egyptian hieroglyphs, and Norse. Using these clues he was able to decipher the language, so reading the *Journal* was easy.

DECORATED LETTERS

The Shepherd's Journal is wonderfully decorated. Many medieval books were decorated with beautiful pictures called illuminations. Monks painstakingly copied out text and painted characters with gold to reflect the glory of God.

Golden letters

*T*HE *Journal gives a detailed map of the route to Atlantis. Every cavern, monster, bridge, and crevice has been noted and explained. With Milo to translate, the crew easily navigates the dark, subterranean pathways to the lost city.*

THE SHEPHERD'S JOURNAL TIMELINE

Hebrew scroll

1000 B.C. The *Journal* is written on a parchment scroll by Aziz, a nomadic shepherd. It is an account of the two years he spent in Atlantis.

c. 600 B.C. The Greek lawgiver and poet Solon thinks that the Scrolls of Aziz are written in the lost language of Atlantis. Much later, Plato reads about Atlantis in Solon's work.

A.D c. 410 Frankish tribes take the Scrolls from Rome to Gaul.

792 The Scrolls are stolen by a fortune hunter, who tries to smuggle them to Iceland. On the way, he becomes ill at Lindesfarne, an island off the coast of England. The island's monk's are entrusted with the Scrolls, which they bind into a book.

793 Vikings plunder Lindesfarne and take the book to Iceland. The *Journal* then goes missing. A secret society is founded, later known as the "Keepers of the *Journal*," to find it and keep it in Iceland.

Viking shield

1499 Portuguese explorer Amerigo Vespucci is given the *Journal* by the Mayan people. They think it is evil and want it removed from their land.

1500 Vespucci gives the *Journal* to his friend Leonardo da Vinci. Da Vinci becomes the first modern man to translate the Atlantean language.

Cambridge University

1589 Pope Sixtus V calls the book, *The Shepherd's Journal*.

1701 English architect Sir Christopher Wren finds the *Journal* in Italy. He lends it to England's Cambridge University.

1778 King Louis XVI of France is given the *Journal*. But it is lost during the French Revolution.

1807 Napoleon's troops discover the *Journal* in Egypt. They are captured by the British Fleet and the *Journal* is taken to the British Museum.

1880 Not believing it to be authentic, the British Museum gives the book to the British Library. It's loaned to an American senator named Ignatious Donelly. Donelly, a "Keeper," smuggles it back to Iceland.

Iceland

1911 Preston B. Whitmore funds an expedition to Iceland to find the *Journal*. Thaddeus Thatch discovers it there and takes it back to the U.S. for study.

ROURKE

A TOUGH-GUY MERCENARY and veteran of many battles, the expedition's commander is not a man to cross. Captain Lyle Tiberius Rourke joined the U.S. Army at 15, where his intelligence and bravery gained him rapid promotion through the ranks. His ruthlessness is legendary—in 1881 he was disciplined for excessive use of force at the Battle of Wounded Knee. He retired from the army in 1901 and eventually embarked on a career with the British Museum, leading expeditions to foreign lands to retrieve priceless artifacts, including *The Shepherd's Journal*.

DURING his mission to Iceland to recover The Shepherd's Journal *in 1911, Rourke's interest was aroused by a page showing the vast Atlantean Crystal. He knew at once this had to be the opportunity of his lifetime, and he devised an evil plan to steal the Crystal for himself.*

Calculating and evil-minded

Wounded seven times in battle

Instructor in hand-to-hand combat

Army uniform

"PLEASURE TO MEET YA"
Rourke greets Milo warmly at the start of the expedition. Milo is instantly at ease, reassured by the fact that Rourke accompanied his grandfather to Iceland. Rourke seems to be a good guy—but is he?

Strong and fit

ROURKE *is a natural leader. He is in his element issuing orders. He expects them to be carried out immediately and to the letter. No questions asked.*

ROURKE'S *patience begins to wear thin with the bumbling dreamer, Milo. Rourke is used to dealing with trained troops. Milo is a whole different ballgame. He can't even drive!*

Boots

TOGETHER, *Helga and Rourke make a formidable pair. They have a long history together, and Rourke thinks nothing of sharing his evil plot with Helga. He can rely on her to help him. She is as coldhearted and ruthless as he is—well, almost.*

RIPPED OUT

Rourke rips the vital page about the Crystal from *The Shepherd's Journal* and keeps it hidden from Milo. But once he is sure that Milo can help him find the gem, he produces the page once more. He needs Milo to translate it.

ROURKE makes his real motive for the trip known to Milo. He thinks the Crystal is a giant diamond, and he wants to take it back with him and sell it for a fortune.

RED MEANS DANGER

Rourke does not care that the Crystal is the power source for Atlantis. The fact that a whole civilization may be destroyed just ups the stakes, in his opinion. But even the Crystal senses his viciousness. It turns a fiery red, sensing that danger is near.

Army revolver

TRUSTY REVOLVER

Rourke likes to have his old Colt .45 at his side at all times. This single-action army revolver has six chambers in its cylinder. Each is loaded with one 0.45-in. (1 cm.) bullets.

ARMY MEDAL

Rourke was awarded the U.S. Army distinguished medal (*left*) during his tour of duty with the Rough Riders, 1888–1901.

KIDA is slowly absorbed into the Crystal. But Rourke's plans don't change. He will take the Crystal no matter what, even if it means kidnapping Kida herself.

EGYPTIAN TREASURE

In 1922, Pharaoh Tutankhamun's Egyptian tomb was opened for the first time in 3,000 years. It contained thousands of golden objects, including the Pharaoh's solid gold coffin (*right*). It had escaped the attention of fortune hunters and looters like Rourke.

THE ULYSSES

MILO SAYS "WOW!" when he gets his first glimpse of the *Ulysses*. The craft was designed by Whitmore Marine Industries, Inc., and built in secret at a high-security dockyard. Its most striking feature is the enormous "bathysphere" at the front. This glass sphere houses the three-level command bridge. The sphere cleverly adjusts so that the bridge stays level, whether the submarine is diving or climbing. It is a marvel of maritime engineering and is years ahead of its time.

THE bathysphere is enormous. It allows the crew unparalleled views from the bridge.

ON THE BRIDGE
Captain Rourke and his lieutenant, Helga, control the craft's operations from the middle bridge. The steersman and second officers sit on the lower bridge. Speakerphones help the crew communicate with each other.

Ballast tanks

Command bridge is on three levels

Gun turrets

Main bridge is on second level

Hull contains 11 capsules on each side from where subpods are launched

Guns fire torpedos and can rotate 180 degrees

Cargo bay houses all other vehicles

EACH member of the crew is assigned a bunk. They are not comfortable. The beds are built into the wall and two people must share each tiny room.

ALL ABOARD

Milo is amazed by the sheer size of the *Ulysses*. It is large enough to carry the full expedition crew of over 200 trained personnel. These include the submarine's engineers, officers, communications corps, pilots, navigators, and, at Rourke's insistence, the troops.

ONCE *the preparations are complete, the* Ulysses *sets sail. Schools of fish watch as the huge submarine slowly begins its long journey to the bottom of the ocean.*

THE *Ulysses' strong searchlights scan the seabed. Little does the crew know what dangers await them in the watery darkness of the Atlantic—dangers beyond their wildest nightmares.*

Stabilizer fin

Aqua-evacs exit from rear of sub

NAUTILUS

The *Ulysses* is inspired by the *Nautilus*, the famous submarine in 20,000 *Leagues Under the Sea*. Published in 1870, the classic tale was written by Jules Verne (1828–1905), a French lawyer. Verne wrote extraordinary adventure stories that transported the reader from the depths of the ocean to the center of the earth.

Periscope

A modern submarine

Galley

Engines

Radio room

UP AND UNDER

Like the *Ulysses*, modern submarines have two large tanks on each side called ballast tanks. These tanks control the depth that the sub cruises at. When they fill with water, the sub goes deeper. When they empty, it surfaces. Rourke works out the direction that the submarine should go by using a type of compass (*right*).

DR. SWEET

THE EXPEDITION'S MEDICAL OFFICER is a big, muscular, gentle man with some remarkable expertise. Joshua Strongbear Sweet was raised with Arapaho Indians in Kansas. While being tutored by his uncle, Iron Cloud, he developed a talent and fascination for alternative medicines and healing practices. After gaining top medical qualifications at college, Sweet went on to lecture at Harvard Medical School. Later he earned high praise as a battlefield surgeon—where he first met Rourke. Rourke then recruited him for the expedition to find *The Shepherd's Journal* in Iceland.

DR. Sweet is very enthusiastic about his medical equipment. He loves to show it off. But poor Milo cannot get excited by the surgical saw—he finds it somewhat intimidating.

6 ft. 6" tall

Army t-shirt

Mountainous physique

Muscular arms

FILL 'EM UP
Straight-talking and to the point, Dr. Sweet goes about his medical duties so fast and efficiently that it's difficult to know when he is joking. "I need you to fill these up," he says, showing Milo two large containers. "With what?" cries Milo in panic. Is this a joke?

Medical bag

Holster

DR. Sweet's father was an army medic, and his mother a Native American. Sweet grew up on various army outposts in the U.S. before his parents settled in Kansas. He is very proud of his mixed heritage.

Stron boots wi waterpro cove

DR. Sweet is the first person to befriend Milo. He invites him to join the team around the campfire, and shares with him some of the wonders of his background.

FATAL MEDICINE

Until the 20th century, many more soldiers died from disease than were killed by their battlefield enemies. Ignorance about the bacterial causes of disease meant that many simple wounds proved fatal because they were not properly cleaned, and dirty instruments were used during surgery.

Medicine bag

OLD PEG LEG

Amputations were frequently carried out on the battlefield. The British Earl of Uxbridge had to lose a leg at the battle of Waterloo in 1815. The Earl survived the surgery and was equipped with an artificial limb. This earned him the nickname "Old Peg–Leg."

Surgeon's saw and glove

MEDICINE POUCH

Army medics like Sweet were often the unsung heroes in a war. Carrying their trusty medicine bags, they ventured onto the battlefields to rescue wounded soldiers and even perform minor surgery.

DR. Sweet puts his Native American medical skills into practice and quickly cracks Milo's aching neck. Milo is surprised by the horrific sound, but his neck feels much better afterward!

WWI medicine pouch

REMEMBERING THADDEUS

Dr. Sweet is the one who is really there for Milo in the hour of his greatest despair. The kindly medic inspires him with a saying of Milo's beloved grandfather: "It's been my experience that when you hit bottom, the only place left to go, is up."

COOKIE

Jebediah Allardyce Farnsworth, or "Cookie," is the chef for the expedition. He likes to work with the "four basic food groups: beans, bacon, whisky, and lard!" A veteran cowpoke cook, whose years on the wagon train have made him the best roadkill chef alive, Cookie is outspoken, and won't put up with insults, especially when it concerns his cuisine. He's the ultimate culinary cowboy, decked out in rubber chest-waders that carry everything, *and* the kitchen sink! Everything Cookie cooks looks gray and greasy. If the crew refuses a second helping, he's not bothered. After all, the stuff will simply "keep and keep and keep!"

Beans

Food's up!

Cowboy meals were no picnic! The cooks were often injured cowboys with no skills, so the food was boring and unhealthy. Hygiene was non–existent—cups and plates were often just thrown into the "wreck pan" and scoured with sand. No wonder once the cowboys reached a town they spent their money on eggs, steaks, and liquor!

On the wagon
Just like Cookie, cowboys had a special wagon that they used to carry all their food supplies and equipment. The very first chuck wagon was designed in 1866.

Chuck wagon

Lard

Bacon

COOKIE does not appreciate Helga's healthy and plentiful food provisions. They are nonessentials in Cookie's opinion.

COOKIE gives Milo an extra-large portion of food. He thinks Milo is way too skinny. "If you turned sideways and stuck out your tongue you'd look like a zipper," he says.

1

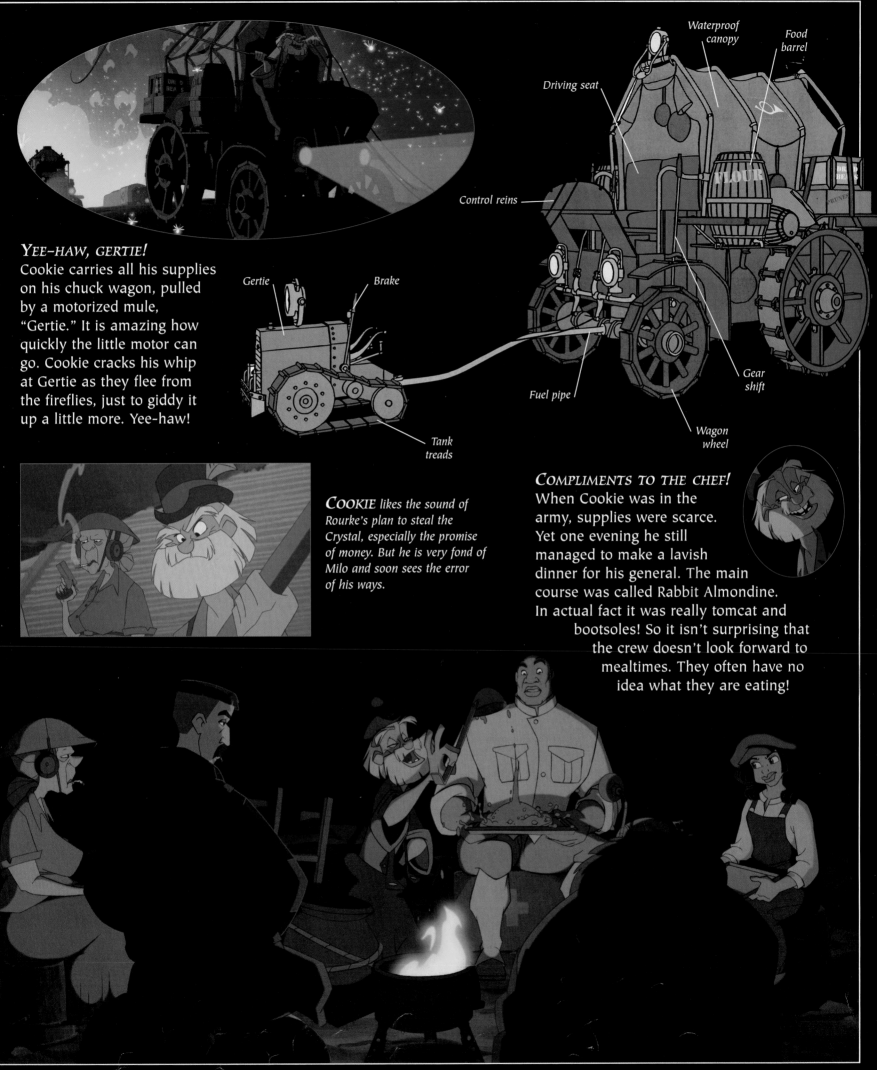

Waterproof canopy

Food barrel

Driving seat

Control reins

FLOUR

YEE-HAW, GERTIE!

Cookie carries all his supplies on his chuck wagon, pulled by a motorized mule, "Gertie." It is amazing how quickly the little motor can go. Cookie cracks his whip at Gertie as they flee from the fireflies, just to giddy it up a little more. Yee-haw!

Gertie

Brake

Fuel pipe

Gear shift

Wagon wheel

Tank treads

COOKIE *likes the sound of Rourke's plan to steal the Crystal, especially the promise of money. But he is very fond of Milo and soon sees the error of his ways.*

COMPLIMENTS TO THE CHEF!

When Cookie was in the army, supplies were scarce. Yet one evening he still managed to make a lavish dinner for his general. The main course was called Rabbit Almondine. In actual fact it was really tomcat and bootsoles! So it isn't surprising that the crew doesn't look forward to mealtimes. They often have no idea what they are eating!

VINNY

VINCENZO SANTORINI IS the demolitions
expert for the expedition. Vinny just
loves to blow stuff up, and he has a
laid-back approach to the highly risky
business of explosives. Surprisingly,
Vinny started out as a florist, but a
massive gas explosion nearly killed him and alerted him to
the fact that flowers weren't his thing. So he followed his
instincts and went into demolitions—by the
age of 18 he was mixing his own formula
for TNT! He's been involved in some
shady dealings in the past, but
now he is on the straight and
narrow, working in the
mining division of
Whitmore Industries.

*VINNY spent some time in Milan's Delphi Prison,
accused of causing an explosion that killed a rival
Italian businessman and four employees. Later
Whitmore busted him out of a Turkish prison.
No prizes for guessing what he was in there for!*

DANGEROUS OFFICE SUPPLIES

Vinny's casual approach to his
demolition equipment shocks Milo.
On their first meeting, Vinny rattles
off the highly dangerous items
he's carrying as if they were
office supplies.

*VINNY and Mole love to play jokes on Milo. When Milo drinks
from the water canteen, Vinny looks horrified, and tells him that it
was nitroglycerin. "Don't move, don't breathe," he warns.
"BOOM!!" shouts Mole. Milo jumps out of his skin!*

*THE Tinder Box belongs to Vinny.
It carries all his explosives, demolition
equipment, and supplies.*

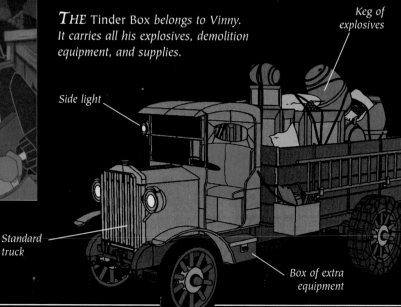

Keg of
explosives

Side light

Standard
truck

Box of extra
equipment

VINNY is always willing to lend a hand when needed. Milo's camping skills are very rusty, but Vinny helps him set up his tent in the caverns.

SANTORINI

Vinny's family takes its name from Santorini, the Greek island that nearly disappeared in a volcanic explosion in 1645 B.C. The explosion supposedly destroyed a whole island. Perhaps this is what led to the myth of Atlantis, an island destroyed in a fiery blast.

CHEST ARMOR
Vinny wears an old fashioned steel breastplate to shield himself against minor blasts. This type of armor was worn in battle during the 1800s.

Sticks of dynamite

Head shaved at the sides

Characteristic laid-back expression

Match

Breastplate

Bag for carrying extra supplies

DYNAMITE ENTRANCE
Initially, Vinny helps Rourke to search for the Crystal. He blasts the doors of a locked room off their hinges.

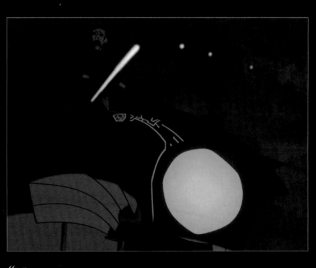

THE detonator is an essential part of Vinny's equipment—he cannot set off those huge explosions without it.

Detonator

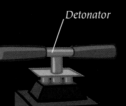

Pants

Stout shoes

"HEY, Milo, you got something sporty, ya know... like a tuna?" Even before battle Vinny keeps his laid-back, casual attitude, as well as his sense of humor!

MOLIÈRE

GAETAN MOLIÈRE, or "Mole," is the expedition's geologist. He's a Frenchman whose primary love and passion in life is dirt. This bizarre interest started at the age of seven, when he began exploring the vast sewer networks beneath Paris. He has a remarkable ability to correctly identify various soils by "taste"—and he can tell a lot about people from the dirt under their fingernails! He is sensitive to light and distrusts those he does not know well. And, what's more, Mole has an iffy diet. According to Audrey he loves to eat roots, burrowing animals, and insects!

MOLIERE has the ability to correctly identify any type of soil without the aid of scientific equipment 98.75% of the time. But his unique set of eyewear helps him to examine and identify extra-fine soils and minerals more easily.

Mole invented this unique headgear and eyewear

Flexible, "hands-free" headlamp

Eyewear adjusters

Leather gloves

Warm, furry collar

Large pockets for tools

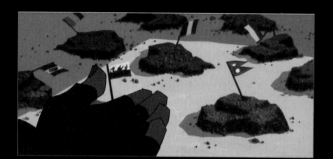

DIRTY HABIT

Some people like to relax by socializing, reading, or playing sports. Mole prefers to organize his dirt samples in the privacy of his room. He is very irritated when Milo disturbs his little collection of muck from around the world. "England must never merge with France!" he exclaims.

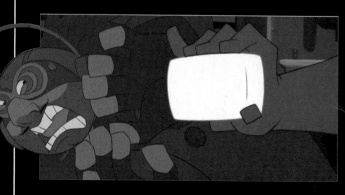

MILO is saved from further harassment by the appearance of Dr. Sweet, who thrusts a bar of soap at the little geologist, warding Mole off as if he were a vampire and the soap was garlic!

Thick, waterproof coat

Hardwearing mining boots

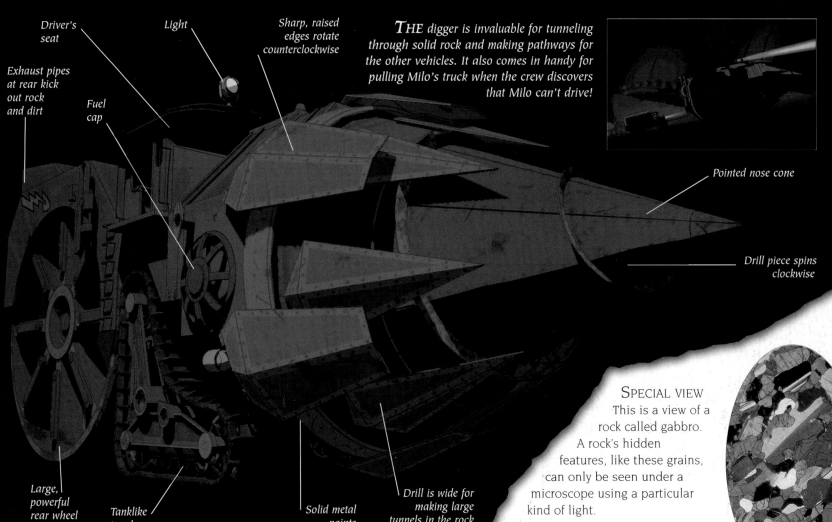

Driver's seat

Light

Sharp, raised edges rotate counterclockwise

Exhaust pipes at rear kick out rock and dirt

Fuel cap

THE digger is invaluable for tunneling through solid rock and making pathways for the other vehicles. It also comes in handy for pulling Milo's truck when the crew discovers that Milo can't drive!

Pointed nose cone

Drill piece spins clockwise

Large, powerful rear wheel

Tanklike treads

Solid metal points

Drill is wide for making large tunnels in the rock

THE DIGGER

While still in his twenties, Mole developed and invented dozens of different vehicles, tools, and related equipment. This digger is his most sophisticated invention to date and was designed exclusively for Whitmore Industries.

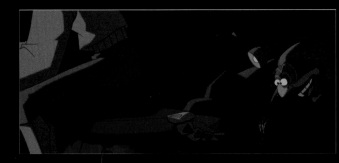

MOLE just can't resist taking the opportunity to play tricks on Milo. A whoopee cushion in Milo's spot by the campfire is a favorite.

MOLE, like the others, is tempted by Rourke's plan. But he soon realizes his mistake, and under Audrey's example finally sides with Milo.

SPECIAL VIEW
This is a view of a rock called gabbro. A rock's hidden features, like these grains, can only be seen under a microscope using a particular kind of light.

MOLE'S EQUIPMENT

A geologist studies rocks, soil, and minerals. His or her basic equipment includes a hammer and a range of chisels. Mole carries these, plus a trowel for digging into soft rocks and a sieve for sorting his collected material. Geologists may also carry paintbrushes for cleaning specimens, spatulas for cutting around fossils, and small boxes for storing the samples.

Magnifying glass

Sample tray

Notebook

Brushes

Trowels

Hammers

MRS. PACKARD

MRS. PACKARD IS THE EXPEDITION'S unflappable communications officer. She's a been-there-seen-it-all, world-weary old widow. Born in 1853 to traveling performers, Wilhelmina Bertha Cudot grew up on the road, and joined the Flora Dora dancing girls when she was 16. She tried several other jobs before her fondness for gossip and eavesdropping took her into the newfangled field of electronic communication devices. In her time, she helped to develop both the concept of the Hertzian Wave application and the vibrating telephone. And she has gone through eight husbands as well!

UNBELIEVABLY, Mrs. Packard was once a pretty, optimistic young girl.

KNOW IT ALL

Mrs. Packard can be very possessive about her position as communications officer. When Mrs. Packard picks up the sound of the Leviathan on the hydrophone, Helga suggests that the sound could be an echo off one of the sunken wrecks. "Do you wanna do my job? Be my guest," retorts Mrs. Packard defensively.

"PACKARD, sound the alarm!"

IT takes a lot to upset Mrs. Packard. Not even the Leviathan crushing the Ulysses worries her. In fact, Helga has to shout at her twice to sound the abandon ship alarm!

MILO is glad of the eyemask Dr. Sweet gives him at the camp—especially when Mrs. Packard informs the crew that she sleeps in the nude and often sleepwalks!

"ARE YOU THERE, MARGE?"

Mrs. Packard has a range of hi-tech communication equipment to use on the expedition. However, she mostly uses it to gossip with her friends. There's nothing she likes better than to settle down with a cup of tea and pass on advice to her long-suffering friend, Marge.

Antenna

Hard hat

Speaker

Painted nails

Antenna

Hydrophone

Army coat

TUBES

BATTERIES
DANGER
ACID

Cargo boxes to sit on

Boots

Cable

MRS. Packard has a witty phrase for every occasion. But as the journey gets more dangerous her favorite one soon becomes, "We're all gonna die!"

MRS. Packard seems to find the whole Atlantis expedition a bit like a vacation. She is forever phoning friends, reading magazines, or taking photographs for her scrapbook. She even manages to find the time and energy in the evening to apply a face mask and put curlers in her hair!

PIGEON POST

In 1914, during World War I, troops in the trenches needed to communicate quickly with one another up and down the front. Messages were sent in many different ways. Radios, runners, trumpet calls, dogs, and pigeons were all used.

Radio headphones

Pigeon message carrier

RADIO HEADPHONES
Italian Guglielmo Marconi (1874–1937) sent the first radio message across the Atlantic in 1901. Regular daily broadcasts started in the U.S. in 1907. Headphones like Mrs. Packard's were needed for listening to the radio in its early days.

AUDREY RAMIREZ

BELIEVE IT OR NOT, the expedition's chief mechanic is a sassy 18-year-old Latina girl named Audrey Rocio Ramirez. An extremely talented mechanic, Audrey could completely take apart and reassemble any clock in the household by the age of 18 months! When she was five, she began working in her father's automobile repair shop as a mechanic's assistant. Later, Audrey thrived in her job at the Henry Ford Automotive Plant. There she began a period of research and invention, where she specialized in gear drives and hydraulics. Quite an unusual life for a young girl in the early 1900s!

AT first Audrey has little patience for the bookish Milo. "Jeez—I used to take lunch money from guys like this," she says with disgust.

DADDY'S GIRL

Audrey's father was the chief mechanic on the expedition to retrieve *The Shepherd's Journal*. Now that he's retired, Audrey expertly takes his place. A talented mechanic, she takes charge of engine room in the *Ulysses*, as well as looking at all the vehicles.

Hat

Long black hair

fashior sl

Dungare

AUDREY'S father had always wanted two sons. Instead he got Audrey and her sister. Between them the girls made him proud—one becoming a boxer and the other a mechanic.

Wrench

Mechanic's gloves

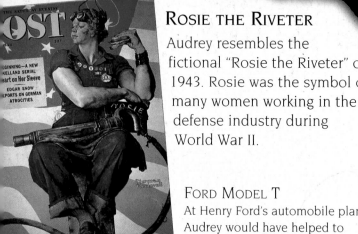

ROSIE THE RIVETER

Audrey resembles the fictional "Rosie the Riveter" of 1943. Rosie was the symbol of many women working in the defense industry during World War II.

Rosie the Riveter

FORD MODEL T

At Henry Ford's automobile plant, Audrey would have helped to make the Model T car. This cheap, tough, and reliable car was first built by Ford in 1908.

Ford Model T

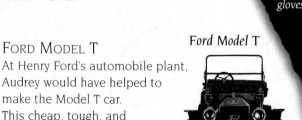

MORE MAINTENANCE

Audrey is in charge of the oiler which carries all the fuel for the expedition. She also makes sure that all the other trucks are in working order. But the constant and extensive maintenance often makes her short-tempered and moody.

ALTHOUGH, like the others, Audrey admits to joining the expedition for money, she can see that Rourke's actions are simply evil, and is the first to join forces with Milo.

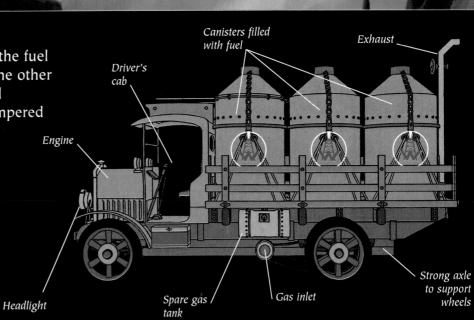

Canisters filled with fuel

Exhaust

Driver's cab

Engine

Headlight

Spare gas tank

Gas inlet

Strong axle to support wheels

SOFT SPOT

Audrey may not have had a lot of time for Milo in the beginning, but later on she develops a soft spot for him. She is very protective of him during their dangerous adventures and is always on hand to help out.

THE LEVIATHAN

Pointed tail for making quick turns and swiping

FOR CENTURIES, sailors have been terrified by tales of the Leviathan. This vast monster is said to live in the depths of the sea, wrecking ships and crushing boats with its giant claws and tentacles. Many civilizations have their own legends of the Leviathan, so when Milo reads a description of a monster guarding the entrance to Atlantis in *The Shepherd's Journal*, he realizes it has to be the same mythical sea serpent. As Milo tries to explain this to the uninterested crew, the sub passes into the Leviathan's lair. The crew barely has time to take in the eerie graveyard of wrecked ships, when Mrs. Packard picks up an alien noise on the hydrophone. Something enormous is heading their way....

IS IT REAL?

The Shepherd's Journal shows an ancient drawing of the Leviathan with the Atlantean words "Enter the lair of the Leviathan, last of the mighty war gods. There you will find the path to the gateway." At first, Milo believes these lines refer to a carving or a sculpture to frighten the superstitious.

Glowing red eye spots the sub

Ulysses

THE bored crew is barely listening to Milo's account of Atlantis's lobster-shaped guardian. When he shows them a drawing of it in The Shepherd's Journal, Vinnie remarks lazily, "With something like that I would have white wine, I think."

Giant claw

THE Leviathan lashes at the submarine, tearing the hull with its massive claws. A giant, red, mechanical eye glares at Milo though the control deck window. "Jiminy Christmas!" he cries. "It's a machine!"

Strong, jointed limb

ELECTRIC CHARGE

The subpods regroup and fire torpedos at the Leviathan. Suddenly, the creature seems to become electrically charged. Its strange markings glow a fluorescent blue, and a massive energy bolt shoots from between its two front claws, blasting a hole straight through the sub!

Sharp hook–shaped claws

Hard, protective shell

Tattoos that glow blue when electrically charged

Mechanical red eye

Small front claw

*acles
en in pods
nd eyes*

*Ulysses is crushed
ae enormous claws*

MONSTERS OF THE DEEP

Food is scarce for deep-sea fish, and they make the most of what they find by having huge mouths and stretchy stomachs, which give them a scary, demonlike appearance. Humans rarely see creatures like these. So it's no wonder that when these deep-sea fish *were* seen, they inspired stories of giant monsters attacking ships.

Angler fish

Giant squid

The Kraken

WHAT A SUCKER!

Some giant squid weigh over a ton. Dead ones are sometimes washed ashore, but no one has ever seen them swimming in the depths.

KRAKEN

A Norwegian story tells of the Kraken, a giant sea monster that wrapped its arms around ships before sinking them. The legend may be based on the mysterious giant squid that live in deep waters.

THE SUBPODS

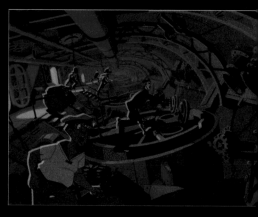

As the Leviathan attacks the *Ulysses*, Rourke orders the launch of the 22 tiny, two-man subpods. Armored and agile, the subpod is a masterpiece of marine engineering. Designed to protect the *Ulysses*, each pod has enough weaponry to sink a battle cruiser! It can operate at incredible depths, but it does have one disadvantage: its lead acid battery can run for only four hours without recharging.

ABANDON SHIP!
At first Rourke is unfazed by the Leviathan: "I want this lobster served up on a silver platter!" But when the beast begins to crack the sub in two, he orders everyone to evacuate.

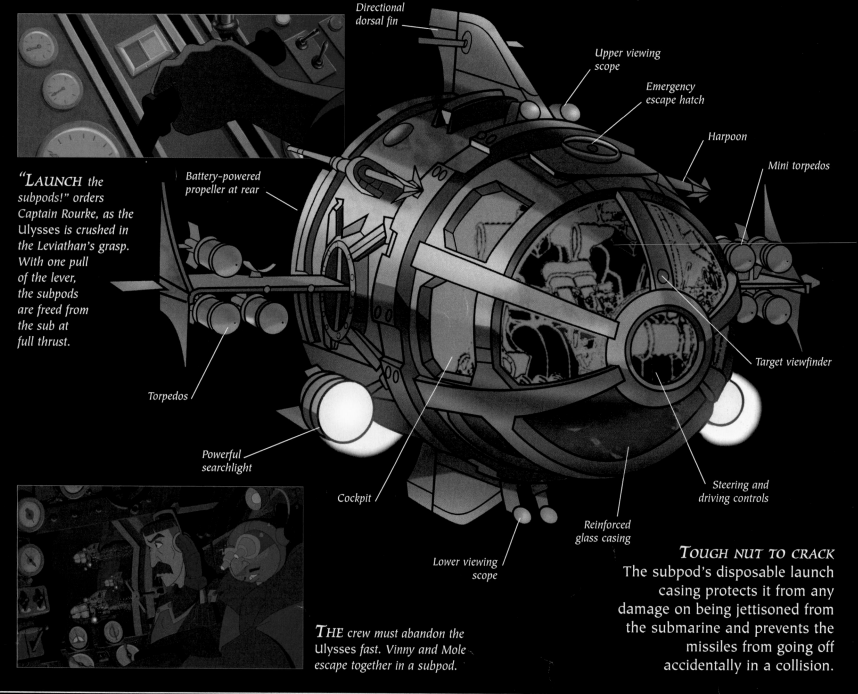

Directional dorsal fin

Upper viewing scope

Emergency escape hatch

Harpoon

Mini torpedos

Battery-powered propeller at rear

"LAUNCH the subpods!" orders Captain Rourke, as the Ulysses is crushed in the Leviathan's grasp. With one pull of the lever, the subpods are freed from the sub at full thrust.

Target viewfinder

Torpedos

Powerful searchlight

Cockpit

Lower viewing scope

Reinforced glass casing

Steering and driving controls

THE *crew must abandon the Ulysses fast. Vinny and Mole escape together in a subpod.*

TOUGH NUT TO CRACK
The subpod's disposable launch casing protects it from any damage on being jettisoned from the submarine and prevents the missiles from going off accidentally in a collision.

THE subpods jettison out of the launching docks of the Ulysses, ready for battle.

ATTACK!

The subpods quickly form a group and launch a powerful attack on the Leviathan. It's a difficult task since the Leviathan fires its own powerful electrical beams. A direct hit can easily destroy a subpod in seconds.

THE subpods bombard the Leviathan with torpedos to save the Ulysses from destruction. Eventually the Leviathan releases it from its grasp.

THE SECRET DEPTHS

The invention of manned underwater vessels (submersibles) allowed the ocean floor to be seen for the first time. But despite modern technology, no one knows what secrets the ocean still holds—for much of it is yet to be explored.

Short mast to renew and expel air with help of bellows

Drill

This early one-man sub was used in the Revolutionary War

Sonar equipment

Titanium sphere protects passengers

Thruster provides power for forward movement

DEEP OCEAN EXPLORER

This modern French submersible is used for marine research. The *Nautile* recovered objects from the seabed surrounding the wreck of the *Titanic*, which lies 2.5 miles (3.8 km.) down. Unlike the subpods, the *Nautile* can stay underwater for up to eight hours.

Video camera

NAUTILE

Nautile measures 26 ft. 6 in. (8 m.) in length

Mechanical arm for picking objects off seabed

Pressurized air containers

AQUA-EVAC

D URING THE LEVIATHAN'S attack, some of the crew escapes in the *Ulysses'* three enormous Aquatic Emergency Evacuation Craft, known as "aqua-evacs." All the expedition's most important equipment is stored in these vessels. They are not armed, but the subpods' barrage of mini torpedos distracts the Leviathan for just long enough to allow the parent vessels time to escape. The aqua-evacs then speed toward a dark tunnel, but only one aqua-evac and one subpod make it to the caverns.

BRUTE FORCE
Helga struggles with a jammed release lever on the aqua-evac. For one tense moment it looks as if the crafts will remain stranded in the exit bay. But Helga is an accomplished karate fighter. With one last kick, the lever moves and the aqua-evacs are ejected.

THE Leviathan's electrical charge strikes the Ulysses, *crippling the sub completely.*

THE aqua-evacs make a bid to escape the Leviathan, dodging the debris of the crushed Ulysses *as they go.*

The monster finally crushes the Ulysses *to pieces with its great claws.*

FEARSOME CRIES

On board the aqua-evac is a very nervous crew—especially Milo! The fearsome shouts from the subpod pilots behind do nothing to help, "We're getting killed out here!"

Searchlight

Propellers at rear

Cockpit

Cargo hold

TERRIFIED Milo
remembers his studies about the secret entrance to Atlantis. "It's only a grease trap," he chants over and over. "It's just like a sink."

Loading hatch

ONE DOWN

The aqua-evacs head through a narrow crevice in the rock, under Milo's guidance. One aqua-evac is lost as it collides with a subpod and smashes into the cave wall. By the time the remaining aqua-evac surfaces in the mysterious cavern, there is only one subpod left to accompany it, carrying Vinny and Mole.

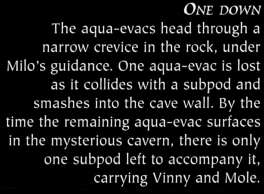

The *Captain Jack*

Crutch wagon

LOST CARGO

One aqua-evac is destroyed, and with it go several important vehicles including the rock saw, crutch wagon, the *Captain Jack*, and the spanner. The crew has to do without these trucks for the rest of the journey. Luckily, the digger was carried on the surviving aqua-evac.

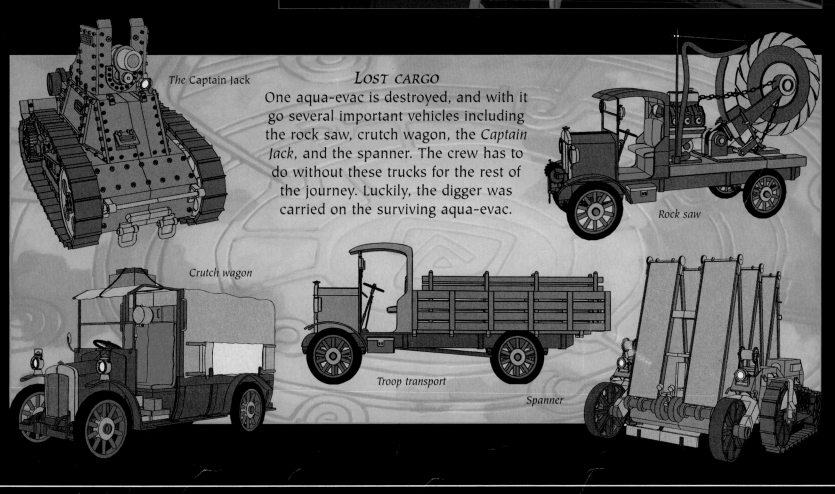

Rock saw

Troop transport

Spanner

THE CAVERNS

THE SURVIVORS OF THE *ULYSSES* COME up for air in a dark, cold cavern. When the aqua-evac's searchlights scan the surrounding blackness, they reveal a huge, carved dragon's head. Milo is speechless. This place must be the greatest archaeological discovery of all time! Then, with some trepidation, the crew turns to face the winding pathway that begins at the dragon's mouth. This is the gateway to the vast subterranean passageways that were once the halls and highways of the Atlantean Empire.

A SWEET TRIBUTE
Despite being at the gateway to Atlantis, the crew cannot forget those lost in battle to the Leviathan. Dr. Sweet lights a candle and floats it in his helmet, as a touchng tribute to their fallen comrades.

MILO LEADS THE WAY
At last the crew needs Milo's mapmaking and language skills. Only an expert in "gibberish" and maps can guide them through the perils and pitfalls of the caverns. "Looks like all our chances rest with you, Mr. Thatch, you and that little book," says Rourke, pointing to *The Shepherd's Journal.*

CITIES OF ROCK
Although a mammoth undertaking, people have carved whole cities from rock. Petra (*left*) is one such place. It can be found in Jordan in the Middle East. It was built 2,000 years ago, and the whole city is carved out of the surrounding sandstone cliffs.

CARVED TEMPLE
This impressive Egyptian temple (*above*) was built thousands of years ago for the king, Ramses II. The temple is hidden behind the statues, deep within the rock.

THE crew stops before a fork in the pathway. After consulting The Shepherd's Journal, Milo points to the path they should take. Seconds later the convoy quickly retreats from the snapping jaws of a giant cave beast. Milo realizes he has been holding the Journal upside down, and quickly rights it. The crew glares at him.

BRIDGING THE GAP

Farther along, the path is blocked by a carved stone pillar hundreds of feet high. "It must have taken hundreds...no, thousands of years to carve this thing!" exclaims Milo. Vinny, however, has no appreciation for ancient sculpture. It takes him only a few seconds to blow it up to make a bridge.

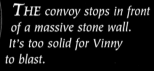

"HEY, look, I made a bridge. And it only took me, what... ten seconds— eleven tops!"

THE convoy stops in front of a massive stone wall. It's too solid for Vinny to blast.

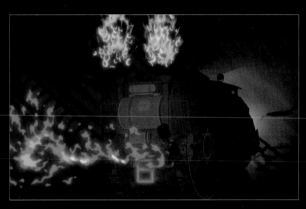

THIS is a job for Mole. He fires up the digger engine and the huge drilling cone begins to bore through the rock.

THE crew sets up camp for the night in front of a slender stone bridge. The whole scene is lit by a strange, glowing rock formation.

PRINCESS KIDA

WILLFUL, HONEST, AND CURIOUS, Kida wants to know more about her world than her father thinks is good for her. She was only a toddler when disaster befell Atlantis and her mother was mysteriously absorbed into the Mother Crystal—a dim memory that still haunts Kida. Kept eternally youthful by the power of the hidden Crystal, Kida is in fact thousands of years old. She has never been able to piece together the truth of why her civilization is dying, until she gets a little help from Milo. Hungry to learn, Kida is an excellent match for Milo, who recognizes in her a kindred spirit. The bond between them quickly grows.

THE convoy of vehicles makes its way through the caverns. High on the nearby cliff, hidden in the shadows, Kida watches. She is curious. Very few outsiders ever make it to Atlantis.

Atlantean spear

Tattoo

Long flowing hair

Crystal life force

A ruthless warrior, Kida has slain outsiders who have tried to enter Atlantis in the past. Strong and fit, Kida can definitely look after herself.

WHAT A PICTURE
Kida finds Milo's satchel containing the photo of him as a little boy with Grandpa Thatch. She studies the photo carefully. Little does she know that the boy in the photo will be the one to help her on her quest to save Atlantis.

AT first, Milo is taken aback by Kida's outfit. In Milo's day, women kept their arms and legs covered.

Brightly colored sarong

Anklets of gold

Royal robes

Strong legs

KIDA is desperate to understand the reason for Atlantis's downfall. Using her personal crystal to light the way, she shows Milo some old underwater murals which she is sure hold a clue to the history of the city. She needs Milo's help to read them since the Atlantean people have lost the ability to read their own language.

KIDA loves her father deeply. There is nothing she wouldn't do for him. Although they may have different expectations for Atlantis, Kida and her father ultimately want the best for their people. Their bond is unbreakable.

KIDA battles with Rourke's troops fearlessly. Strong and agile, she is quite a match for them.

BATTLE OF WILLS
Kida may be able to outmaneuver Rourke's troops, but she has no chance once she is captured. Holding her tightly, Helga shows the princess no mercy.

KIDA'S crystal necklace glows brightly as the giant Crystal chooses her to save the city. Kida knows that she faces the same fate as her mother, but she is not afraid. She doesn't even think of herself, taking time to tell Milo not to worry.

THAI MOVES
Some of Kida's fighting moves are similar to Thai boxing. This ancient art of fighting allows kicks, knee strikes, and elbow strikes. It is all about kicking and punching very hard. Punch bags and impact pads are used to develop power, timing, and the ability to judge distances.

Thai boxers

Statue of Boadicea

WARRIOR QUEEN
Warrior women like Kida have been known throughout history. Thousands of years ago, the Celtic people of Western Europe were greatly feared. They were a noble and warlike race, whose women fought alongside men. The most famous Celt was Boadicea. She was a Celtic queen who led her people in a war against the Romans.

Crystal

HEALING POWER
Many people believe that crystals have special energies that can be harnessed and used to aid healing.

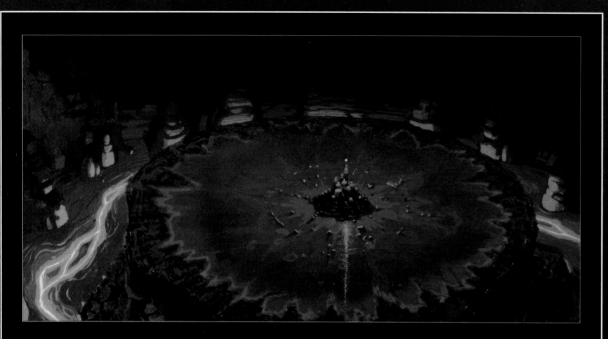

Atlantis is not the dusty archaeological ruin that the team thought would exist. It is a living, functioning civilization. No wonder the sight of it leaves Milo speechless with amazement! But the most sensational discovery is yet to come. For what strange power source could possibly be sustaining life in a city that hasn't seen the sun in thousands upon thousands of years?

THE KING

KING KASHEKIM NEDAKH ruled Atlantis at the time the city sank below the waves, and still rules it. He is over 20,000 years old and feels the burden of the ages weighing down upon him. He had to lose his wife to save the city and witness Atlantis's downfall. Now, blind and careworn, he lives only for Kida's love and his duty to protect the Atlanteans from the truth about their past. Over the centuries the king has allowed his people to lose their ability to read. He is aware that knowledge can enlighten, but believes it can also destroy.

DESPITE Rourke's polite request for the crew to stay in Atlantis for one night, the king does not readily oblige. He does not approve of the fact that they have weapons with them and makes it very clear that they are not welcome.

PROTECTIVE PARENT
The king is fiercely protective of his people, and he does not trust intruders. Although he allows the crew to remain in Atlantis for a night, he is careful to remind Kida of the rule, "No outsiders may see the city and live."

MILO cannot tell Rourke where the Crystal is. So Rourke asks the king.

"MAYBE ol' King Cole here can help us fill in the blanks."

THE king may be blind and weak, but his will is strong. He is not intimidated by Rourke. He will not tell Rourke where the Crystal is.

Coos

Sightless eyes

Royal staff

Gourd

Decorative panels

ROURKE punches the king in anger. The king falls to the ground. The punch is just too much for the frail man to take. What little strength he has slowly seeps away. Dr. Sweet rushes to the king's aid.

THE king knows he does not have long to live. Not even the healing crystals can help him now.

ROYAL SECRET

The king trusts Milo. He shares with him the secret of the Crystal's power, how he misused it and then tried to hide it from his people. In his dying breath, he sets Milo an enormous task. "Return the Crystal, save the city, save my daughter..."

Statue of Poseidon

SEA KING

In Greek mythology, Poiseidon was the ruler of the sea. A powerful god, he had a magnificent underwater palace. The first ten kings of Atlantis were all Poseidon's sons. Maybe King Kashekim Nedakh is a distant relative.

STORED IN A GOURD

The king has tied three special pouches to his staff, called gourds. Gourds have been used for thousands of years. They can be used to store anything from water to poison! The king uses his to store his own personal crystals.

Gourd

ILO is saddend by the death of the king l losing Kida to the Crystal. The king's den now rests heavily on his shoulders.

KIDA'S HIDEOUT

KIDA IS VERY WORRIED about her empire's dying culture and its crumbling walls. She knows that Milo is clever, and thinks that he will be able to help her understand more about Atlantis's past. She trusts Milo enough to take him to her secret hideout. There they learn more about each other's people, and Milo gets his first glimpse of the wondrous Atlantean technology. But a far more exciting discovery is yet to come....

WHILE Milo tries to pluck up the cour to ask Kida more about Atlantis, K surprises him. "I have some questions you, and you are not leaving the city u they are answered." Milo can only mun his okay before she grabs his arm a leads him aw

KIDA
pushes a rock aside, revealing the entrance to an overgrown cave filled with tools and statues. It's her secret hideout.

*"*You *are a scholar, are you not? Judging from your diminished physic and large forehead, you are suited f nothing else!"*

SHOW–AND–TELL
Once in the cave, Kida and Milo take turns asking each other questions. Kida is anxious to know how Milo and the crew found the lost city. So Milo shows Kida *The Shepherd's Journal* that led them to Atlantis.

KIDA stares at The Shepherd's Journal. She is puzzled. She cannot understand how Milo can read it. None of the Atlantean people can read their own language.

KIDA uncovers a big stone fish. "It looks like some kind of vehicle," says Milo. But Kida cannot get it to work. Even placing a hand on the inscription pad does nothing.

Tail acts like a rudder

Driver's seat

Aerodynamic fins

Headlight

HOW DOES IT WORK?

Together Milo and Kida study the Atlantean instructions on the stone fish. After inserting Kida's special crystal into it, and turning the crystal with a hand on the inscription pad, the fish jumps into action. It hovers above the ground, glowing blue. When Milo touches it, it shoots off around the room, sending Milo and Kida diving for cover.

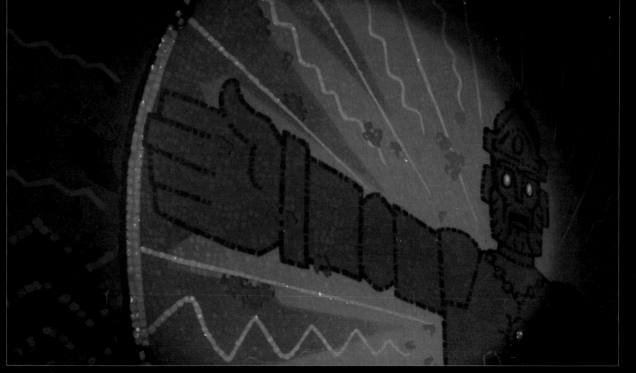

KIDA has more secrets to share with Milo. They swim out into the water surrounding the city and then dive beneath. There lie the flooded ruins of ancient Atlantean buildings. Their walls are covered with fantastic murals which show Atlantis's history and tell the story of a giant Crystal. Suddenly Milo realizes that this mystery gem is very important.

THE CRYSTAL CHAMBER

MILO AND KIDA emerge from the water after their exciting discovery, to the extended hand of Rourke. He wants Milo to tell him where the Crystal is hidden, using the stolen page from *The Shepherd's Journal*. However, the Crystal's location is only described by a riddle. Rourke and Milo struggle to answer it, not realizing that they are closer to the Crystal than they think. For nearby under the water of a pool in the King's palace lies a special "aquavator," marked by the Atlantean "A" symbol. It could just take them where they want to go.

MILO bumps his head on the cave wall as he rushes to the surface to explain the murals' meaning to Kida. The bright light that whisked away her mother was actually from a giant Crystal. It is the Atlantean power source, keeping everything and everyone alive!

HIDDEN DEPTHS
Unknown to Milo and the crew, the Crystal has been hidden by the king in a special chamber within the palace. He does not want Kida to suffer the same fate as his wife, and so he has made sure that it is almost impossible to find. Only the missing page from *The Shepherd's Journal* holds a clue to its whereabouts.

ROURKE helps Milo out of the water after his swim. He needs Milo to guide him and the crew to the Crystal. Little does Rourke know that he is nearer to it than he realizes.

MILO is shocked to find that all of the crew have been in on Rourke's plan. Rourke has promised them that they will be rich if they help him find and sell the Crystal.

"*THE* *Heart of Atlantis lies within the eyes of her king,*" is the one clue the stolen page gives to the Crystal's location. Suddenly the answer dawns on Rourke. He begins to smile.

ROURKE *heads for a pool of water. In the middle of the pool is the Atlantean "A" symbol marked by rocks. As Helga, Milo, Kida, and Rourke step onto the symbol, the water begins to vibrate. Then the symbol starts to descend like an elevator, taking the crew with it into the unknown...*

"*JACKPOT!*"

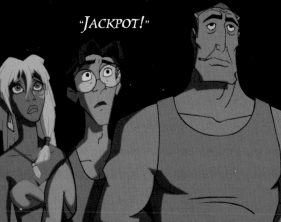

AT LAST
The aquavator comes to a halt. The crew step off it into the Chamber of the Kings. There they see The Heart of Atlantis, floating high above a pool of water. Its powerful blue light fills the cavern.

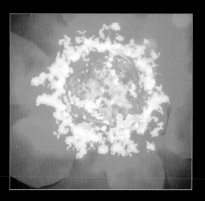

NOTHING
can prepare Rourke,
Helga, Milo, and Kida for the
sight of the Crystal—the Heart
of Atlantis.

STONES AND CRYSTALS

TENS OF THOUSANDS OF YEARS AGO, a cometlike Crystal fell to earth on the empire of Atlantis. It possessed extraordinary powers, which the people soon learned to harness. But the king misjudged this power and used the Crystal as a weapon of war. The Crystal's power proved too great to control. It overwhelmed and destroyed Atlantis. After the catastrophe the king kept the Crystal hidden, and over the centuries he allowed his people to forget it ever existed. Despite this, the Crystal continued to protect and nourish Atlantis. It is the Atlanteans' life force. Without it they will die.

King Kashekim Nedakh's face can clearly be seen on this stone

Markings glow blue with Crystal power

THE KING STONES

The 10 king stones orbit protectively around the Crystal. Each is carved symbolically with depictions of former kings of Atlantis. They are suspended in the air by the Crystal's power.

"OHH...the kings of our past!"

KIDA *is overwhelmed by the carved king stones, which glow blue. She falls to her knees in prayer.*

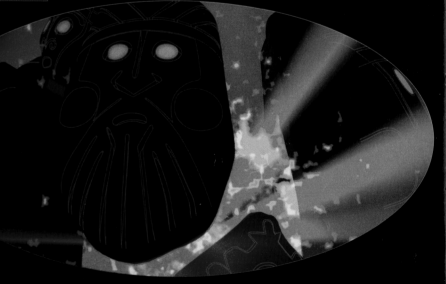

ROURKE *kicks a stone into the pool beneath the Crystal. Suddenly, the blue light from the Crystal changes to fiery red as it senses evil. It sends out search beams through the chamber, in an attempt to find a royal host.*

THE ROYAL HOST

In times of danger, the Crystal chooses a "host," one of royal blood, to protect itself and its people. This time it chooses Kida, just as it chose her mother years before. She is lifted into the air, toward the Crystal's core. The king stones revolve around her very quickly.

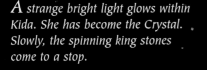

ON the ground, Rourke, Milo, and Helga gaze up at Kida in wonder. Milo consults the Journal and tries to explain it. The Crystal is the Atlanteans' power source. They are part of it and it is part of them.

A strange bright light glows within Kida. She has become the Crystal. Slowly, the spinning king stones come to a stop.

KIDA floats back to the ground. As she does so the king stones crash down into the water around her. When she walks ashore, Rourke reaches out to her. Milo knows better. "No, don't! Don't touch her!" he cries.

FROM SAPPHIRE TO RUBY

The Crystal—also called the Heart of Atlantis—changes color dramatically from a cool blue to fiery red the moment it senses danger. This echoes the colors of the two most beautiful gemstones, sapphires and rubies.

Colorful gems

Earth crystal

CRYSTALS EVERYWHERE

Crystals are all around us. We live on a crystal planet. The rocks that form the earth, moon, and meteorites are made up of minerals, and nearly all of these minerals are made up of crystals.

MILO THE HERO

ROURKE AND HELGA kidnap the crystallized princess. Now their plan to steal the Crystal is nearly complete. Milo feels responsible for this as the map reader who, in his own words, led a "band of plundering vandals" straight to the greatest archaeological discovery of all time. But the crisis brings out in him one thing that he never knew he had: courage. Taking the king's dying wish to heart—to save the city and Princess Kida—Milo knows he must do the right thing. Full of anger and determination, he unites the Atlanteans and the explorers against Rourke and Helga.

ROURKE and Helga have rigged the bridge. It will blow up, stopping anyone following the pair to the volcano, where they will make their escape in the gyro-evac balloon. There's just one thing they haven't bargained for... the heroic Milo Thatch!

THE LAST STRAW

As Rourke gets ready to escape from Atlantis, he throws an unexpected punch at Milo. Milo is knocked to the ground. This is the last straw for him. A new, more courageous Milo starts to emerge.

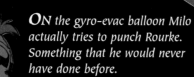

ON the gyro-evac balloon Milo actually tries to punch Rourke. Something that he would never have done before.

"WELL, I have to hand it to you. You're a bigger pain in the neck than I would have ever thought possible."

MILO'S picture of his grandfather is smashed into pieces by Rourke. Watching the scuffle, the rest of the crew knows that what Rourke is doing is wrong. One by one they join Milo.

STRONG MAN

Milo sets out to rescue Kida. Luckily the pod carrying her drops from the gyro-evac balloon. But the balloon itself is on fire and is rapidy hurtling toward the ground. With a newfound strength, Milo pushes the huge heavy pod out of the way of the balloon just before it lands in a massive explosion.

MILO quickly attaches the pod by a chain to a flying fish. Now the crew can pull it to safety. But the chain is not strong enough, and as the flying fish begins to gather speed, the chain breaks. The princess is in danger once more.

INTO THE FLAMES

Milo jumps off the stone fish after the pod that carries Kida, ignoring the cries from Audrey that it is too dangerous. Dodging the lava and flames, Milo hooks a chain around the pod and holds on. "Go!" he shouts. The fish lifts off carrying Kida to safety. Who would have thought that Milo had this kind of courage? There is no stopping this unexpected hero!

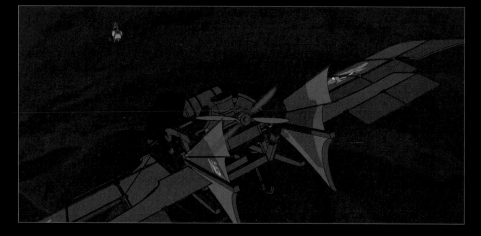

Milo leads the Atlanteans and the explorers in the battle against Rourke's troops. It is an awesome sight. The Atlanteans and the crew shoot the blue energy blasts from their stone fish. The troops in the Whitmore Wing airplanes fight back, firing their own shots at the unusual and agile stone vehicles, with little success!

GYRO-EVAC

THE TEAM KNOWS NOTHING of the escape balloon secretly stored inside the tanker until they see it carrying Rourke and Helga upward through the dormant volcano. Rourke has attached the princess pod by a chain and is using the gyro-evac to float out of Atlantis. Now it's just Rourke and his prize. The Atlantean armada and Milo are close to stopping Rourke's evil plan, but the craft is finally destroyed by a direct shot from Helga's flare gun. The flammable gas inside the balloon ignites and brings it crashing to the ground.

HELGA and Rourke race to the big, red gyro-evac balloon with the princess. It is the perfect way for them to escape from Atlantis.

MY BEAUTIFUL BALLOON
The gyro-evac is self-inflated with hydrogen. Its motorized propeller gives it an accelerated lift. The attached pod makes an excellent prison cell for the crystallized Kida.

UP, UP, AND AWAY
Airships made the first intercontinental passenger flights, and were a popular form of transportation until the 1930s, when the German airship *Hindenburg* exploded killing those on board.

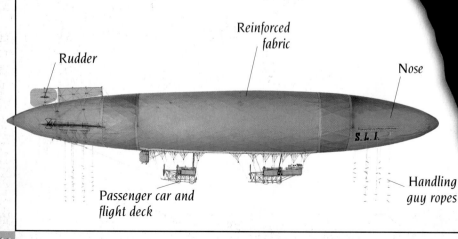

Rudder

Reinforced fabric

Nose

S.L.I.

Passenger car and flight deck

Handling guy ropes

"LADIES first..."

WHEN the balloon starts to lose height, Rourke turns on Helga. They start to fight. As Helga kicks him away, he catches her foot, twists it, and throws her over the side for good.

Hydrogen
canisters

Inflated
balloon

GOING DOWN

Milo swings his way from chain to chain to reach Rourke. Rourke climbs down toward him. Rourke breaks a glass container which holds an ax and swings it madly at Milo. Missing Milo, he smashes the window of the princess pod. Glass shards lie everywhere, glowing blue with the Crystal energy.

ROURKE heads for the volcano opening. But Milo is hot on his heels.

Milo
climbs
the chain

Propeller

HELGA lies on the ground, barely alive after her fall from the balloon. She summons the last of her anger-fueled energy and grasps her flare gun. With an effort she fires the flare at Rourke and the balloon. "Nothing personal," she whispers as the flare shoots up into the sky.

Crystal
Kida is
trapped
in the
pod

Chain for
pod

Princess
pod

THE balloon catches fire. As Rourke makes his way toward Milo with the ax, Milo grabs a piece of glass still glowing with Crystal energy. He slices Rourke's arm. Rourke's arm—then body—crystallize, turning black and red. Then the propeller hits Rourke's crystal body, smashing it to smithereens. Milo jumps from the balloon just before it hits the ground in a ball of fire.

THE STONE GIANTS

ONCE AGAIN THE EMPIRE OF ATLANTIS is in danger as the volcano erupts and its molten lava begins to flow. But this empire has some very special guardians—the Stone Giants. These giant statues are buried under the water around Atlantis, huge pieces of forgotten, carved stone. But when the Crystal's powerful light falls on them, they rumble into life, energized by the beams. Once standing, they form a circle around the city, and begin to clap their hands. The clapping creates a huge dome of blue energy, which spreads like a canopy over the empire, saving it from danger and destruction.

The tallest Giant is 101 ft. high

Eyes light up with Crystal energy

Tattoos

Tattoos glow blue when brought to life

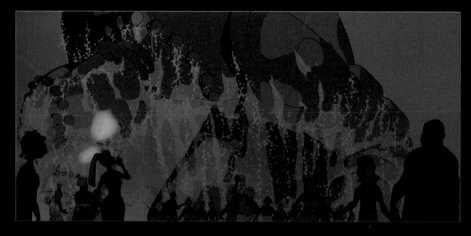

GIANTS ARISE
The Crystal's beams scan the city, and come to rest on the Stone Giants. Now they are brought to life and rise from the water, glowing with power.

Clapping creates the protective dome

Atlantean stone containing traces of granite

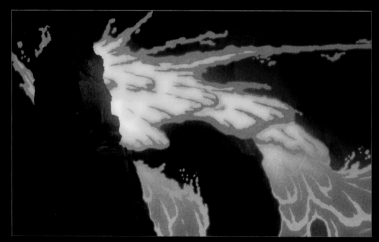

THE volcano starts to erupt. Once again Atlantis is threatened with destruction. Soon the volcanic lava is breaking through the empire walls!

CLAP YOUR HANDS

The lava threatens to engulf the city, but the Stone Giants are now on their feet and they start to clap. The huge blue spheres of energy created by the clapping form an enormous dome over the whole of the city.

THE underground empire is suddenly lit up by the waves of molten lava —a river of fire.

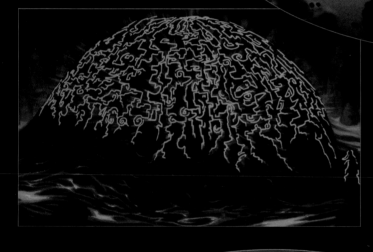

THE lava flows engulf the city, but the protective dome the Stone Giants created holds firm. The lava then quickly cools and hardens. Then it cracks in a glowing mosaic and falls away. Atlantis is saved once again.

STONE GIANT

This huge "giant" can be found in Leshan in China. It stands 233 feet tall. It was carved by monks and it took 72 years to complete. It is the largest Buddha statue in the world.

KIDA floats down into Milo's arms. The steam from the lava hitting the water clears, to reveal a different, more beautiful Atlantis than ever before.

GIANT HEADS

Stone heads such as these have been found on the Gulf Coast of Mexico. They were made thousands of years ago by the ancient Olmec people. It is thought they may be the heads of ballgame players, or possibly "portraits" of rulers or chiefs.

61

And so the crew returns to Mr. Whitmore's mansion once more. All are present in his study, except Helga, Rourke, and... Milo! Milo has decided to stay in Atlantis with Kida. He doesn't forget Mr. Whitmore. Milo sends him a photo of himself and Kida, along with a crystal necklace—just to prove Atlantis really exists. "I'm sure gonna miss that boy," sighs Mr. Whitmore, but he smiles as he places the necklace around his neck.

The secret of Atlantis is safe from the outside world once more....

Dorling Kindersley

LONDON, NEW YORK, SYDNEY, DEHLI, PARIS,
MUNICH, and JOHANNESBURG.

WRITTEN BY DAVID JOHN

EDITOR REBECCA KNOWLES

SENIOR DESIGNER ROBERT PERRY

DESIGNER GOLDY BROAD

PUBLISHING MANAGER CYNTHIA O'NEILL

ART DIRECTOR CATHY TINCKNELL

U.S. EDITOR GARY WERNER

SENIOR DTP DESIGNER ANDREW O'BRIEN

PRODUCTION NICOLA TORODE

PICTURE RESEARCHER ANGELA ANDERSON

PICTURE LIBRARIANS

SALLY HAMILTON, RICHARD DABB, DIANE LE GRANDE

First American Edition, 2001
00 01 02 03 04 05 10 9 8 7 6 5 4 3 2 1
Published in the United States by
Dorling Kindersley Publishing, Inc.
95 Madison Avenue
New York, New York 10016

Library of Congress Cataloging-in-Publication Data
John, David.
Atlantis, the Lost Empire, 2001 : the essential guide / [David John].
    p. cm.
    ISBN 0-7894-7334-8
    1. Atlantis, the Lost Empire (Motion picture)--Juvenile literature.
[1. Atlantis, the Lost Empire (Motion picture)]   I. Title.
PN1997.A848 J64 2001
791.43'72--dc21
    00-065703

Reproduced by MDP, England
Printed and bound by World Color, USA

Dorling Kindersley would like to thank:
Eric Huang, Hunter Heller, Lori Heiss, Deirdre Cutter, Rachel Alor,
Tim Lewis, Graham Barnard, and Victoria Saxon at Disney
Publishing; Troy Knutson, Don Hahn, Kirk Wise, James Russell, Joe
Pfenning, and Gary Trousdale at Walt Disney Feature Animation.

The publisher would like to thank the following for their kind
permission to reproduce their images:
t = top b = bottom c = center l = left r = right
Royal Geographical Society: 9 tr, cr; Popperfoto: 9 br; Mary Evans Picture Library:
Pach 15 tr, Denys de Montfort 35 br; British Library: 16 bl, 17 tl; The Viking Society of
Great Britain: 17 bl; Robin Wigington, Arbour Antiques: 19 tr; Andrew L. Chernack:
19 cr; National Army Museum: 23 cr; Imperial War Museum: 23 br; Breastplate © The
Wallace Collection: 27 br; University College London: 29 tr; Science Museum: 31 br,
58 bl; Peter Newark's American Pictures: 32 tl; Stephen Oliver: 43 br; Ken Robertson
Collection: 61 tr; Demetrio Carrasco - Museo de Antropologia de Xalapa: 61 br.

Additional photography by: Max Alexander, Geoff Brightling, Tina Chambers, Andy
Crawford, Geoff Dan, Alistair Duncan, David Exton, Frank Greenaway, Colin Keates,
Dave King, Mick Loates, Roger Phillips, Rob Reichenfeld, Jane Stockman, Clive Streeter,
and Linda Whitwam.

For our complete catalog visit
www.dk.com